BLACK CANAAN

BY

ROBERT E. HOWARD

British Library Cataloguing-in-Publication Data
A catalogue record for this book is available from the
British Library

Contents

Robert E. Howard

Robert Ervin Howard was born in Peaster, Texas in 1906. During his youth, his family moved between a variety of Texan boomtowns, and Howard – a bookish and somewhat introverted child – was steeped in the violent myths and legends of the Old South. Although he loved reading and learning, Howard developed a distinctly Texan, hardboiled outlook on the world. He became a passionate fan of boxing, taking it up at an amateur level, and from the age of nine began to write adventure tales of semi-historical bloodshed. In 1919, when Howard was thirteen, his family moved to the Central Texas hamlet of Cross Plains, where he would stay for the rest of his life.

At fifteen Howard began to read the pulp magazines of the day, and to write more seriously. The December 1922 issue of his high school newspaper featured two of his stories, 'Golden Hope Christmas' and 'West is West'. In 1924 he sold his first piece – a short caveman tale titled 'Spear and Fang' – for $16 to the not-yet-famous *Weird Tales* magazine. He published with the magazine regularly over the next few years. 1929 was a breakout year for Howard, in that the 23-year-old writer began to sell to other magazines, such as *Ghost Stories* and *Argosy*, both of whom had previously sent him hundreds of rejection slips. In 1930, he began a correspondence with weird fiction master H. P. Lovecraft which ran up to his death six years later, and is regarded as one of the great correspondence cycles in all of fantasy literature.

It was partly due to Lovecraft's encouragement that Howard created his most famous character, Conan the Cimmerian. Conan – a barbarian-turned-King during the Hyborian Age, a mythical period of some 12,000 years ago – featured in seventeen *Weird Tales* stories between 1933 and 1936, and is now regarded as having spawned the 'sword and sorcery' genre, making Howard's influence on fantasy literature comparable to that of J. R. R. Tolkien's. The Conan stories have since been adapted many times, most famously in the series of films starring Arnold Schwarzenegger.

Howard was enjoying an all-time high in sales by the beginning of 1936, but he was also deeply upset by the ill health of his mother, who had fallen into a coma. On the morning of June 11, 1936, he asked an attending nurse whether she would ever recover, and the nurse replied negatively. Howard walked to his car, parked outside the family home in Cross Plains, and shot himself. He died eight hours later, aged just thirty.

CALL FROM CANAAN

"Trouble on Tularoosa Creek!" A warning to send cold fear along the spine of any man who was raised in that isolated back-country, called Canaan, that lies between Tularoosa and Black River-to send him racing back to that swamp-bordered region, wherever the word might reach him.

It was only a whisper from the withered lips of a shuffling black crone, who vanished among the throng before I could seize her; but it was enough. No need to seek confirmation; no need to inquire by what mysterious, black-folk way the word had come to her. No need to inquire what obscure forces worked to unseal those wrinkled lips to a Black River man. It was enough that the warning had been given-and understood.

Understood? How could any Black River man fail to understand that warning? It could have but one meaning-old hates seething again in the jungle-deeps of the swamplands, dark shadows slipping through the cypress, and massacre stalking out of the black, mysterious village that broods on the moss-festooned shore of sullen Tularoosa.

Within an hour New Orleans was falling further behind me with every turn of the churning wheel. To every man born in Canaan, there is always an invisible tie that draws him back whenever his homeland is imperiled by the murky shadow that has lurked in its jungled recesses for more than half a century.

The fastest boats I could get seemed maddeningly slow for that race up the big river, and up the smaller, more turbulent stream. I was burning with impatience when I stepped off on the Sharpsville landing, with the last fifteen miles of my journey yet to make. It was past midnight, but I hurried to the livery stable where, by tradition half a century old, there is always a Buckner horse, day or night.

As a sleepy black boy fastened the cinches, I turned to the owner of the stable, Joe Lafely, yawning and gaping in the light of the lantern he upheld. "There are rumors of trouble on Tularoosa?"

He paled in the lantern-light.

"I don't know. I've heard talk. But you people in Canaan are a shut-mouthed clan. No one outside knows what goes on in there."

The night swallowed his lantern and his stammering voice as I headed west along the pike.

The moon set red through the black pines. Owls hooted away off in the woods, and somewhere a hound howled his ancient wistfulness to the night. In the darkness that foreruns dawn I crossed Nigger Head Creek, a streak of shining black fringed by walls of solid shadows. My horse's hooves splashed through the shallow water and clinked on the wet stones, startlingly loud in the stillness. Behind Nigger Head Creek began the countrymen called Canaan

Heading in the same swamp, miles to the north, that gives birth to Tularoosa, Nigger Head flows due south to ioin Black River a few miles west of Sharpsville, while the Tularoosa runs westward to meet the same river at a higher point. The trend of Black River is from northwest to southeast; so these three streams form the great irregular triangle known as Canaan.

In Canaan lived the sons and daughters of the white frontiersmen who first settled the country, and the sons and daughters of their slaves. Joe Lafely was right; we were an isolated, shut-mouthed breed. Self-sufficient, jealous of our seclusion and independence.

Beyond Nigger Head the woods thickened, the road narrowed, winding through unfenced pinelands, broken by live-oaks and cypresses. There was no sound except the soft clop-clop of hoofs in the thin dust, the creak of the saddle. Then someone laughed throatily in the shadows.

I drew up and peered into the trees. The moon had set and dawn was not yet come, but a faint glow quivered among the trees, and by it I made out a dim figure under the moss-hung branches. My hand instinctively sought the butt of one of the dueling-pistols I wore, and the action brought another low, musical laugh, mocking yet seductive.

I glimpsed a brown face, a pair of scintillant eyes, white teeth displayed in an insolent smile.

"Who the devil are you?" I demanded.

"Why do you ride so late, Kirby Buckner?" Taunting laughter bubbled in the voice. The accent was foreign and unfamiliar; a faintly negroid twang was there, but it was rich and sensuous as the rounded body of its owner. In the lustrous pile of dusky hair a great white blossom glimmered palely in the darkness.

"What are you doing here?" I demanded. "You're a long way from any darky cabin. And you're a stranger to me.

"I came to Canaan since you went away," she answered. "My cabin is on the Tularoosa. But now I've lost my way. And my poor brother has hurt his leg and cannot walk."

"Where is your brother?" I asked, uneasily. Her perfect English was disquieting to me, accustomed as I was to the dialect of the black folk.

"Back in the woods, there-far back!" She indicated the black depths with a swaying motion of her supple body rather than a gesture of her hand, smiling audaciously as she did so.

I knew there was no injured brother, and she knew I knew it, and laughed at me. But a strange turmoil of conflicting emotions stirred in me. I had never before paid any attention to a black or brown woman. But this quadroon girl was different from any I had ever seen. Her features were regular as a white woman's, and her speech was not that of a common wench. Yet she was barbaric, in the open lure of her smile, in the gleam of her eyes, in the shameless posturing of her voluptuous body. Every gesture, every motion she made set her apart from the ordinary run of women; her beauty was untamed and lawless, meant to madden rather than to soothe, to make a man blind and dizzy, to rouse in him all the unreined passions that are his heritage from his ape ancestors.

I hardly remember dismounting and tying my horse. My blood pounded suffocatingly through the veins in my temples as I scowled down at her, suspicious yet fascinated.

"How do you know my name? Who are you?"

With a provocative laugh, she seized my hand and drew me deeper into the shadows. Fascinated by the lights gleaming in her dark eyes, I was hardly aware of her action.

"Who does not know Kirby Buckner?" she laughed. "All the people of Canaan speak of you, white or black. Come! My poor brother longs to look upon you!" And she laughed with malicious triumph.

It was this brazen effrontery that brought me to my senses. Its cynical mockery broke the almost hypnotic spell in which I had fallen.

I stopped short, throwing her hand aside, snarling: "What devil's game are you up to, wench?"

Instantly the smiling siren was changed to a blood-mad jungle cat. Her eyes flamed murderously, her red lips writhed in a snarl as she leaped back, crying out shrilly. A rush of bare feet answered her call. The first faint light of dawn struck through the branches, revealing my assailants, three gaunt black giants. I saw the gleaming whites of their eyes, their bare glistening teeth, the sheen of naked steel in their hands.

My first bullet crashed through the head of the tallest man, knocking him dead in full stride. My second pistol snapped-the cap had somehow slipped from the nipple. I dashed it into a black face, and as the man fell, half stunned, I whipped out my bowie knife and closed with the other. I parried his stab and my counter-stroke ripped across the belly-muscles. He screamed like a swamp-panther and made a wild grab for my knife wrist, but I stuck him in the mouth with my clenched left fist, and felt his lips split and his teeth crumble under the impact as he reeled backward, his knife waving wildly. Before he could regain his balance I was after him, thrusting, and got home under his ribs. He groaned and slipped to the ground in a puddle of his own blood.

I wheeled about, looking for the other. He was just rising, blood streaming down his face and neck. As I started for him he sounded a panicky yell and plunged into the underbrush. The crashing of his blind flight came back to me, muffled with distance. The girl was gone.

THE STRANGER ON TULAROOSA

The curious glow that had first showed me the quadroon girl had vanished. In my confusion I had forgotten it. But I did not waste time on vain conjecture as to its source, as I groped my way back to the road. Mystery had come to the pinelands and a ghostly light that hovered among the trees was only part of it.

My horse snorted and pulled against his tether, frightened by the smell of blood that hung in the heavy damp air. Hoofs clattered down the road, forms bulked in the growing light. Voices challenged.

"Who's that? Step out and name yourself, before we shoot!"

"Hold on, Esau!" I called. "It's me--Kirby Buckner'"

"Kirby Buckner, by thunder!" ejaculated Esau McBride, lowering his pistol. The tall rangy forms of the other riders loomed behind him.

"We heard a shot," said McBride. "We was ridin' patrol on the roads around Grimesville like we've been ridin' every night for a week now--ever since they killed Ridge Jackson."

"Who killed Ridge Jackson?"

"The swamp niggers. That's all we know. Ridge come out of the woods early one mornin' and knocked at Cap'n

Sorley's door. Cap'n says he was the color of ashes. He hollered for the Cap'n for God's sake to let him in, he had somethin' awful to tell him. Well, the Cap'n started down to open the door, but before he'd got down the stairs he heard an awful row among the dogs outside, and a man screamed he reckoned was Ridge. And when he got to the door, there wasn't nothin' but a dead dog layin' in the yard with his head knocked in, and the others all goin' crazy. They found Ridge later, out in the pines a few hundred yards from the house. From the way the ground and the bushes was tore up, he'd been dragged that far by four or five men. Maybe they got tired of haulin' him along. Anyway, they beat his head into a pulp and left him layin' there."

"I'll be damned!" I muttered. "Well, there's a couple of niggers lying back there in the brush. I want to see if you know them. I don't."

A moment later we were standing in the tiny glade, now white in the growing dawn. A black shape sprawled on the matted pine needles, his head in a pool of blood and brains. There were wide smears of blood on the ground and bushes on the other side of the little clearing, but the wounded black was gone.

McBride turned the carcass with his foot.

"One of them niggers that came in with Saul Stark," he muttered.

"Who the devil's that?" I demanded.

"Strange nigger that moved in since you went down the river last time. Come from South Carolina, he says. Lives in that old cabin in the Neck-you know, the shack where Colonel Reynolds' niggers used to live."

"Suppose you ride on to Grimesville with me, Esau, "' I said, "and tell me about this business as we ride. The rest of you might scout around and see if you can find a wounded nigger in the brush."

The agreed without question; the Buckners have always been tacitly considered leaders in Canaan, and it came natural for me to offer suggestions. Nobody gives orders to white men in Canaan.

"I reckoned you'd be showin' up soars," opined McBride, as we rode along the whitening road. "You usually manage to keep up with what's happenin' in Canaan."

"What is happening?" I inquired. "I don't know anything. An old black woman dropped me the word in New Orleans that there was trouble. Naturally I came home as fast as I could. Three strange niggers waylaid me-" I was curiously disinclined to mention the woman. "And now you tell me somebody killed Ridge Jackson. What's it all about?"

"The swamp niggers killed Ridge to shut his mouth," announced McBride. "That's the only way to figure it. They must have been close behind him when he knocked on Cap'n Sorley's door. Ridge worked for Cap'n Sorley most of his life; he thought a lot of the old man. Some kind of deviltry's bein' brewed up in the swamps, and Ridge wanted to warn the Cap'n. That's the way I figure it."

"Warn him about what?"

"We don't know," confessed McBride. "That's why we're all on edge. It must be an uprisin'."

That word was enough to strike chill fear into the heart of any Canaan-dweller. The blacks had risen in 1845, and the red terror of that revolt was not forgotten, nor the three lesser rebellions before it, when the slaves rose and spread fire and slaughter from Tularoosa to the shores of Black River. The fear of a black uprising lurked for ever in the depths of that forgotten back-country; the very children absorbed it in their cradles.

"What makes you think it might be an uprising?" I asked.

"The niggers have all quit the fields, for one thing. They've all got business in Goshen. I ain't seen a nigger nigh Grimesville for a week. The town niggers have pulled out."

In Canaan we still draw a distinction born in antebellum days. "Town niggers are descendants of the houseservants of the old days, and most of them live in or near Grimesville There are not many, compared to the mass of "swamp niggers" who dwell on tiny farms along the creeks and the edge of the swamps, or in the black village of Goshen, on the Tularoosa. They are descendants of the field-hands of other days, and, untouched by the mellow civilization which refined the natures of the house-servants, they remain as primitive as their African ancestors."

"Where have the town niggers gone?" I asked.

"Nobody knows. They lit out a week ago. Probably hidin' down on Black River. If we win, they'll come back. If we don't, they'll take refuge in Sharpsville."

I found his matter-of-factness a bit ghastly, as if the actuality of the uprising were an assured fact.

"Well, what have you done?" I demanded.

"Ain't much we could do," he confessed. "The niggers ain't made no open move, outside of killin' Ridge Jackson; and we couldn't prove who done that, or why they done it.

"They ain't done nothin' but clear out. But that's mighty suspicious. We can't keep from thinkin' Saul Stark's behind it."

"Who is this fellow?" I asked.

"I told you all I know, already. He got permission to settle in that old deserted cabin on the Neck; a great big black devil that talks better English than I like to hear a nigger talk. But he was respectful enough. He had three or four big South Carolina bucks with him, and a brown wench which we don't know whether she's his daughter, sister, wife or What. He ain't been in to Grimesville but that one time, and a few weeks after he came to Canaan, the niggers begun actin' curious. Some of the boys wanted to

13

ride over to Goshen and have a show-down, but that's takin' a desperate chance."

I knew he was thinking of a ghastly tale told us by our grandfathers of how a punitive expedition from Grimesville was once ambushed and butchered among the dense thickets that masked Goshen, then a rendezvous for runaway slaves, while another red-handed band devastated Grimesville, left defenseless by that reckless invasion.

"Might take all the men to get Saul Stark," said McBride. "And we don't dare leave the town unprotected. But we'll soon have to-hello, what's this?"

We had emerged from the trees and were just entering the village of Grimesville, the community center of the white population of Canaan. It was not pretentious. Log cabins, neat and whitewashed, were plentiful enough. Small cottages clustered about big, old-fashioned houses which sheltered the rude aristocracy of that backwoods democracy. All the "planter" families lived "in town." "The country" was occupied by their tenants, and by the small independent farmers, white and black.

A small log cabin stood near the point where the road wound out of the deep forest. Voices emanated from it, in accents of menace, and a tall lanky figure, rifle in hand, stood at the door.

"Howdy, Esau!" this man hailed us. "By golly, if it ain't Kirby Buckner! Glad to see you, Kirby."

"'What's up, Dick?" asked McBride.

"Got a nigger in the shack, tryin' to make him talk. Bill Reynolds seen him sneakin' past the edge of town about daylight, and nabbed him."

"Who is it?" I asked.

"Tope Sorley. John Willoughby's gone after a blacksnake."

With a smothered oath I swung off my horse and strode in, followed by McBride. Half a dozen men in boots and gunbelts clustered about a pathetic figure cowering on an old broken bunk. Tope Sorley (his forebears had adopted the name of the family that owned them, in slave days) was a pitiable sight just then. His skin was ashy, his teeth chattered spasmodically, and his eyes seemed to be trying to roll back into his head.

"Here's Kirby!" ejaculated one of the men as I pushed my way through the group. "I'll bet he'll make this coon talk!"

"Here comes John with the blacksnake!" shouted someone, and a tremor ran through Tope Sorley's shivering body.

I pushed aside the butt of the ugly whip thrust eagerly into my hand.

"Tope," I said, "you've worked one of my father's farms for years. Has any Buckner ever treated you any way but square?"

"Nossuh," came faintly.

"Then what are you afraid of? Why don't you speak up? Something's going on in the swamps. You know, and I want you to tell us why the town niggers have all run away, why Ridge Jackson was killed, why the swamp niggers are acting so mysteriously."

"And what kind of devilment that cussed Saul Stark's cookin' up over on Tularoosa!" shouted one of the men.

Tope seemed to shrink into himself at the mention of Stark.

"I don't dast," he shuddered. "He'd put me in de swamp!"

"Who?" I demanded. "Stark? Is Stark a conjer man?"

Tope sank his head in his hands and did not answer. I laid my hand on his shoulder.

"Tope," I said, "you know if you'll talk, we'll protect you. If you don't talk, I don't think Stark can treat you much rougher than these men are likely to. Now spill it—what's it all about?"

He lifted desperate eyes.

"You-all got to lemme stay here," he shuddered. "And guard me, and gimme money to git away on when de trouble's over."

"We'll do all that," I agreed instantly. "You can stay right here in this cabin, until you're ready to leave for New Orleans or wherever you want to go."

He capitulated, collapsed, and words tumbled from his livid lips.

"Saul Stark's a conjer man. He come here because it's way off in back-country. He aim to kill all de white folks in Canaan-"

A growl rose from the group, such a growl as rises unbidden from the throat of the wolf-pack that scents peril.

"He aim to make hisself king of Canaan. He sent me to spy dis mornin' to see if Mistah Kirby got through. He sent men to waylay him on de road, cause he knowed Mistah Kirby was comin' back to Canaan. Niggers makin' voodoo on Tularoosa, for weeks now. Ridge Jackson was goin' to tell Cap'n Sorley; so Stark's niggers foller him and kill him. That make Stark mad. He ain't want to kill Ridge; he want to put him in de swamp with Tunk Bixby and de others."

"What are you talking about?" I demanded.

Far out in the woods rose a strange, shrill cry, like the cry of a bird. But no such bird ever called before in Canaan. Tope cried out as if in answer, and shriveled into himself. He sank down on the bunk in a veritable palsy of fear.

"That was a signal!" I snapped. "Some of you go out there."

Half a dozen men hastened to follow my suggestion, and I returned to the task of making Tope renew his revelations. It was useless. Some hideous fear had sealed his lips. He lay shuddering like a stricken animal, and did not even seem to hear our questions. No one suggested the use of the blacksnake. Anyone could see the Negro was paralyzed with terror.

Presently the searchers returned empty-handed. They had seen no one, and the thick carpet of pine needles showed no foot-prints. The men looked at me expectantly. As Colonel Buckner's son, leadership was expected of me.

"What about it, Kirby?" asked McBride. "Breckinridge and the others have just rode in. They couldn't find that nigger you cut up."

"There was another' nigger I hit with a pistol," I said. "Maybe he came back and helped him. "Still I could not bring myself to mention the brown girl. "Leave Tope alone. Maybe he'll get over his scare after a while. Better keep a guard in the cabin all the time. The swamp niggers may try to get him as they got Ridge Jackson. Better scour the roads around the town, Esau; there may be some of them hiding in the woods."

"I will. I reckon you'll want to be gettin' up to the house, now, and seein' your folks."

"Yes. And I want to swap these toys for a couple of .44s. Then I'm going to ride out and tell the country people to come into Grimesville. If it's to be an uprising, we don't know when it will commence."

"You're not goin' alone!" protested McBride.

"I'll be all right," I answered impatiently. "All this may not amount to anything, but it's best to be on the safe side. That's why I'm going after the country folks. No, I don't want anybody to go with me. Just in case the niggers do get crazy enough to attack the town, you'll need every man you've got. But if I can get hold of some of the swamp niggers and talk to them, I don't think there'll be any attack."

"You won't get a glimpse of them," McBride predicted

SHADOWS OVER CANAAN

It was not yet noon when I rode out of the village westward along the old road. Thick woods swallowed me quickly. Dense walls of pines marched with me on either hand, giving way occasionally to fields enclosed with straggling rail fences, with the log cabins of the tenants or owners close by, with the usual litters of tow-headed children and lank hound dogs.

Some of the cabins were empty. The occupants, if white, had already gone into Grimesville; if black they had gone into the swamps, or fled to the hidden refuge of the town niggers, according to their affiliations. In any event, the vacancy of their hovels was sinister in its suggestion.

A tense silence brooded over the pinelands, broken only by the occasional wailing call of a plowman. My progress was not swift, for from time to time I turned off the main road to give warning to some lonely cabin huddled on the bank of one of the many thicket-fringed creeks. Most of these farms were south of the road; the white settlements did not extend far to the north; for in that direction lay Tularoosa Creek with its jungle-grown marshes that stretched inlets southward like groping fingers.

The actual warning was brief; there was no need to argue or explain. I called from the saddle: "Get into town; trouble's brewing on Tularoosa." Faces paled, and people dropped whatever they were doing: the men to grab guns and jerk mules from the plow to hitch to the wagons, the women to bundle necessary belongings together and shrill the children in from their play. As I rode I heard the cowhorns blowing up and down the creeks, summoning men from distant fields-blowing as they had not blown for a generation, a warning and a defiance which I knew carried to such ears as might be listening in the edges of the swamplands. The country emptied itself behind me, flowing in thin but steady streams toward Grimesville.

The sun was swinging low among the topmost branches of the pines when I reached the Richardson cabin, the westernmost "white" cabin in Canaan. Beyond it lay the Neck, the angle formed by the junction of Tularoosa with Black River, a jungle-like expanse occupied only by scattered Negro huts.

Mrs. Richardson called to me anxiously from the cabin stoop.

"Well, Mr. Kirby, I'm glad to see you back in Canaan! We been hearin' the horns all evenin', Mr. Kirby. What's it mean? It--it ain't--"

"You and Joe better get the children and light out for Grimesville," I answered. "Nothing's happened yet, and may not, but it's best to be on the safe side. All the people are going."

"We'll go right now!" she gasped, paling, as she snatched off her apron. "Lord, Mr. Kirby, you reckon they'll cut us off before we can git to town?"

I shook my head. "They'll strike at night, if at all. We're just playing safe. Probably nothing will come of it."

"I bet you're wrong there," she predicted, scurrying about in desperate activity. "I been hearin' a drum beatin' off toward Saul Stark's cabin, off and on, for a week now. They beat drums back in the Big Uprisin'. My pappy's told me about it many's the time. The nigger skinned his brother alive. The horns was blowin' all up and down the creeks, and the drums was beatin' louder'n the horns could blow. You'll be ridin' back with us, won't you, Mr. Kirby?"

"No; I'm going to scout down along the trail a piece."

"Don't go too far. You're liable to run into old Saul Stark and his devils. Lord! Where is that man? Joe! Joe!"

As I rode down the trail her shrill voice followed me, thin-edged with fear.

Beyond the Richardson farm pines gave way to liveoaks. The underbrush grew ranker. A scent of rotting vegetation impregnated the fitful breeze. Occasionally I sighted a nigger hut, half hidden under the trees, but always it stood silent and deserted. Empty nigger cabins meant but one thing: the blacks were collecting at Goshen, some miles to the east on the Tularoosa; and that gathering, too, could have but one meaning.

My goal was Saul Stark's hut. My intention had been formed when I heard Tope Sorley's incoherent tale. There could be no doubt that Saul Stark was the dominant figure in this web of mystery. With Saul Stark I meant to deal. That I might be risking my life was a chance any man must take who assumes the responsibility of leadership.

The sun slanted through the lower branches of the cypresses when I reached it-a log cabin set against a background of gloomy tropical jungle. A few steps beyond it began the uninhabitable swamp in which Tularoosa emptied its murky current into Black River. A reek of decay hung in the air; gray moss bearded the trees, and poisonous vines twisted in rank tangles.

I called: "Stark! Saul Stark! Come out here!"

There was no answer. A primitive silence hovered over the tiny clearing. I dismounted, tied my horse and approached the crude, heavy door. Perhaps this cabin held a clue to the mystery of Saul Stark; at least it doubtless contained the implements and paraphernalia of his noisome craft. The faint breeze dropped suddenly. The stillness became so intense it was like a physical impact. I paused, startled; it was as if some inner instinct had shouted urgent warning.

As I stood there every fiber of me quivered in response to that subconscious warning; some obscure, deep-hidden instinct sensed peril, as a man senses the presence of the rattlesnake in the darkness, or the swamp panther crouching in the bushes. I drew a pistol, sweeping the trees and bushes, but saw no shadow or movement to betray the ambush I feared. But my instinct was unerring; what I sensed was not lurking in the woods about me; it was inside the cabin-waiting. Trying to shake off the feeling, and irked by a vague half-memory that kept twitching at the back of my brain, I again advanced. And again I stopped short, with one foot on the tiny stoop, and a hand half advanced to pull open the door. A chill shivering swept over me, a sensation like that which shakes a man to whom a flicker of lightning has revealed the black abyss into which another blind step would have hurled him. For the first time in my life I knew the meaning of fear; I knew that black horror lurked in that sullen cabin under the moss-bearded cypresses-a horror against which every primitive instinct that was my heritage cried out in panic.

And that insistent half-memory woke suddenly. It was the memory of a story of how voodoo men leave their huts guarded in their absence by a powerful ju-ju spirit to deal madness and death to the intruder. White men ascribed such deaths to superstitious fright and hypnotic suggestion. But in that instant I understood my sense of lurking peril; I comprehended the horror that breathed like an invisible mist from that accursed hut. I sensed the reality of the ju-ju, of which the grotesque wooden images which voodoo men place in their huts are only a symbol.

Saul Stark was gone; but he had left a Presence to guard his hut.

I backed away, sweat beading the backs of my hands. Not for a bag of gold would I have peered into the shuttered windows or touched that unbolted door. My pistol hung in my hand, useless I knew against the Thing in that cabin. What it was I could not know, but I knew it was some brutish, soulless entity drawn from the black swamps by the spells of voodoo. Man and the natural animals are not the only sentient beings that haunt this planet. There are invisible Things-black spirits of the deep swamps and the slimes of the river beds-the Negroes know of them...

My horse was trembling like a leaf and he shouldered close to me as if seeking security in bodily contact. I mounted and reined away, fighting a panicky urge to strike in the spurs and bolt madly down the trail.

I breathed an involuntary sigh of relief as the somber clearing fell away behind me and was lost from sight. I did not, as soon as I was out of sight of the cabin, revile myself for a silly fool. My experience was too vivid in my mind. It was not cowardice that prompted my retreat from that empty hut; it was the natural instinct of self-preservation, such as keeps a squirrel from entering the lair of a rattlesnake.

My horse snorted and shied violently. A gun was in my hand before I saw what had startled me. Again a rich musical laugh taunted me.

25

She was leaning against a bent tree-trunk, her hands clasped behind her sleek head, insolently posing her sensuous figure. The barbaric fascination of her was not dispelled by daylight; if anything, the glow of the lowhanging sun enhanced it.

"Why did you not go into the ju-ju cabin, Kirby Buckner?" she mocked, lowering her arms and moving insolently out from the tree.

She was clad as I had never seen a swamp woman, or any other woman, dressed. Snakeskin sandals were on her feet, sewn with tiny sea-shells that were never gathered on this continent. A short silken skirt of flaming crimson molded her full hips, and was upheld by a broad beadworked girdle. Barbaric anklets and armlets clashed as she moved, heavy ornaments of crudely hammered gold that were as African as her loftily piled coiffure. Nothing else she wore, and on her bosom, between her arching breasts, I glimpsed the faint lines of tattooing on her brown skin.

She posed derisively before me, not in allure, but in mockery. Triumphant malice blazed in her dark eyes; her red lips curled with cruel mirth. Looking at her then I found it easy to believe all the tales I had heard of torture and mutilations inflicted by the women of savage races on wounded enemies. She was alien, even in this primitive setting; she needed a grimmer, more bestial background, a background of steaming jungle, reeking black swamps, flaring fires and cannibal feasts, and the bloody altars of abysmal tribal gods.

"Kirby Buckner!" She seemed to caress the syllables with her red tongue, yet the very intonation was an obscene insult. "Why did you not enter Saul Stark's cabin? It was not locked! Did you fear what you might see there? Did you fear you might come out with your hair white like an old man's, and the drooling lips of an imbecile?"

"What's in that hut?" I demanded.

She laughed in my face, and snapped her fingers with a peculiar gesture.

"One of the ones which come oozing like black mist out of the night when Saul Stark beats the ju-ju drum and shrieks the black incantation to the gods that crawl on their bellies in the swamp."

"What is he doing here? The black folk were quiet until he came."

Her red lips curled disdainfully. "Those black dogs? They are his slaves. If they disobey he kills them, or puts them in the swamp. For long we have looked for a place to begin our rule. We have chosen Canaan. You whites must go. And since we know that white people can never be driven away from their land, we must kill you all."

It was my turn to laugh, grimly.

"They tried that, back in '05."

27

"They did not have Saul Stark to lead them, then," she answered calmly.

"Well, suppose they won? Do you think that would be the end of it? Other white men would come into Canaan and kill them all."

"They would have to cross water," she answered. "We can defend the rivers and creeks. Saul Stark will have many servants in the swamps to do his bidding. He will be king of black Canaan. No one can cross the waters to come against him. He will rule his tribe, as his fathers ruled their tribes in the Ancient Land."

"Mad as a loon!" I muttered. Then curiosity impelled me to ask: "Who is this fool? What are you to him?"

"He is the son of a Kongo witch-finder, and he is the greatest voodoo priest out of the Ancient Land," she answered, laughing at me again. "I? You shall leant who I am, tonight in the swamp, in the House of Damballah."

"Yes?" I grunted. "What's to prevent me from taking you into Grimesville with me? You know the answers to questions I'd like to ask."

Her laughter was like the slash of a velvet whip.

"You drag me to the village of the whites? Not all death and hell could keep me from the Dance of the Skull, tonight in the House of Damballah. You are my captive, already." She laughed derisively as I started and glared into the shadows about me. "No one is hiding there. I am alone, and you are the strongest man in Canaan. Even Saul Stark fears you, for he sent me with three men to kill you before you could reach the village. Yet you are my captive. I have but to beckon, so"--she crooked a contemptuous finger--"and you will follow to the fires of Damballah and the knives of the torturers."

I laughed at her, but my mirth rang hollow. I could not deny the incredible magnetism of this brown enchantress; it fascinated and impelled, drawing me toward her, beating at my will power. I could not fail to recognize it any more than I could fail to recognize the peril in the ju-ju hut.

My agitation was apparent to her, for her eyes flashed with unholy triumph.

"Black men are fools, all but Saul Stark," she laughed. "White men are fools, too. I am the daughter of a white man, who lived in the but of a black king and mated with his daughters. I know the strength of white men, and their weakness. I failed last night when I met you in the woods, but now I cannot fail!" Savage exultation thrummed in her voice. "By the blood in your veins I have snared you. The knife of the man you killed scratched your handseven drops of blood that fell on the pine needles have given me your soul! I took that blood, and Saul Stark gave me the man who ran away. Saul Stark hates cowards. With his hot, quivering heart, and seven drops of your blood, Kirby Buckner, deep in the swamps I have made such magic as none but the Bride of Damballah can make. Already you feel its urge! Oh, you are strong! The man you fought with the knife died less than an hour later. But you cannot fight me. Your blood makes you my slave. I have put a conjurment upon you."

By heaven, it was not mere madness she was mouthing! Hypnotism, magic, call it what you will, I felt its onslaught on my brain and will-a blind, senseless impulse that seemed to be rushing me against my will to the brink of some nameless abyss.

"I have made a charm you cannot resist!" she cried. "When I call you, you will come! Into the deep swamps you will follow me. You will see the Dance of the Skull and you will see the doom of a poor fool who sought to betray Saul Stark-who dreamed he could resist the Call of Damballah when it came. Into the swamp he goes tonight, with Tunk Bixby and the other four fools who opposed Saul Stark. You shall see that. You shall know and understand your own doom. And then you too shall go into the swamp, into darkness and silence deep as the darkness of nighted Africa! But before the darkness engulfs you there will be sharp knives, and little fires-oh, you will scream for death, even for the death that is beyond death!"

With a choking cry I whipped out a pistol and leveled it full at her breast. It was cocked and my finger was on the trigger. At that range I could not miss. But she looked full into the black muzzle and laughed-laughed-laughed, in wild peals that froze the blood in my veins.

And I sat there like an image pointing a pistol I could not fire! A frightful paralysis gripped me. I knew, with numbing certainty, that my life depended on the pull of that trigger, but I could not crook my finger-not though every muscle in my body quivered with the effort and sweat broke out on my face in clammy beads.

She ceased laughing, then, and stood looking at me in a manner indescribably sinister.

"You cannot shoot me, Kirby Buckner," she said quietly. "I have enslaved your soul. You cannot understand my power, but it has ensnared you. It is the Lure of the Bride of Damballah-the blood I have mixed with the mystic waters of Africa drawing the blood in your veins. Tonight you will come to me, in the House of Damballah."

"You lie!" My voice was an unnatural croak bursting from dry lips. "You've hypnotized me, you she-devil, so I can't pull this trigger. But you can't drag me across the swamps to you."

"It is you who lie," she returned calmly. "You know you lie. Ride back toward Grimesville or wherever you will Kirby Buckner. But when the sun sets and the black shadows crawl out of the swamps, you will see me beckoning you, and you will follow me. Long I have planned your doom, Kirby Buckner, since first I heard the white men of Canaan talking to you. It was I who sent the word down the river that brought you back to Canaan. Not even Saul Stark knows of my plans for you.

"At dawn Grimesville shall go up in flames, and the heads of the white men will be tossed in the blood-running streets. But tonight is the Night of Damballah, and a white sacrifice shall be given to the black gods. Hidden among the trees you shall watch the Dance of the Skull-and then I shall call you forth-to die! And now, go fool! Run as far and as fast as you will. At sunset, wherever you are, you will turn your footsteps toward the House of Damballah!"

And with the spring of a panther she was gone into the thick brush, and as she vanished the strange paralysis dropped from me. With a gasped oath I fired blindly after her, but only a mocking laugh floated back to me.

Then in a panic I wrenched my horse about and spurred him down the trail. Reason and logic had momentarily vanished from my brain, leaving me in the grasp of blind primitive fear. I had confronted sorcery beyond my power to resist. I had felt my will mastered by the mesmerism in a brown woman's eyes. And now one driving urge overwhelmed me-a wild desire to cover as much distance as I could before that low-hanging sun dipped below the horizon and the black shadows came crawling from the swamps.

And yet I knew I could not outrun the grisly specter that menaced me. I was like a man fleeing in a nightmare, trying to escape from a monstrous phantom which kept pace with me despite my desperate speed.

I had not reached the Richardson cabin when above the drumming of my flight I heard the clop of hoofs ahead of me, and an instant later, sweeping around a kink in the trail, I almost rode down a tall, lanky man on an equally gaunt horse.

He yelped and dodged back as I jerked my horse to its haunches, my pistol presented at his breast.

"Look out, Kirby! It's me-Jim Braxton! My God, you look like you'd seen a ghost! What's chasin' you?"

"Where are you going?" I demanded, lowering my gun.

"Lookin' for you. Folks got worried as it got late and you didn't come in with the refugees: I 'lowed I'd light out and look for you. Miz Richardson said you rode into the Neck. Where in tarnation you been?"

"To Saul Stark's cabin."

"You takin' a big chance. What'd you find there?"

The sight of another white man had somewhat steadied ray nerves. I opened my mouth to narrate my adventure, and was shocked to hear myself saying, instead: "Nothing. He wasn't there."

"Thought I heard a gun crack, a while ago," he remarked, glancing sharply at me sidewise.

"I shot at a copperhead," I answered, and shuddered. This reticence regarding the brown woman was compulsory; I could no more speak of her than I could pull the trigger of the pistol aimed at her. And I cannot describe the horror that beset me when I realized this. The conjer spells the black men feared were not lies, I realized sickly; demons in human form did exist who were able to enslave men's will and thoughts.

Braxton was eyeing me strangely.

"We're lucky the woods ain't full of black copperheads," he said. "Tope Sorley's pulled out."

"What do you mean?" By an effort I pulled myself together.

"Just that. Tom Breckinridge was in the cabin with him. Tope hadn't said a word since you talked to him. Just laid on that bunk and shivered. Then a kind of holler begun way out in the woods, and Tom went to the door with his rifle-gun, but couldn't see nothin'. Well, while he was standin' there he got a lick on the head from behind, and as he fell lie seen that craxy nigger Tope jump over him and light out for the woods. Tom he taken a shot at him, but missed. Now what do you make of that?"

"The Call of Damballah!" I muttered, a chill perspiration beading my body. "God! The poor devil!"

"Huh? What's that?"

34

"For God's sake let's not stand here mouthing! The sun will soon be down!" In a frenzy of impatience I kicked my mount down the trail. Braxton followed me, obviously puzzled. With a terrific effort I got a grip on myself. How madly fantastic it was that Kirby Buckner should be shaking in the grip of unreasoning terror! It was so alien to my whole nature that it was no wonder Jim Braxton was unable to comprehend what ailed me.

"Tope didn't go of his own free will," I said. "That call was a summons he couldn't resist. Hypnotism, black magic, voodoo, whatever you want to call it, Saul Stark has some damnable power that enslaves men's willpower. The blacks are gathered somewhere in the swamp, for some kind of a devilish voodoo ceremony, which I have reason to believe will culminate in the murder of Tope Sorley. We've got to get to Grimesville if we can. I expect an attack at dawn."

Braxton was pale in the dimming light. He did not ask me where I got my knowledge.

"We'll lick 'em when they come; but it'll be slaughter."

I did not reply. My eyes were fixed with savage intensity on the sinking sun, and as it slid out of sight behind the trees I was shaken with an icy tremor. In vain I told myself that no occult power could draw me against my will. If she had been able to compel me, why had she not forced me to accompany her from the glade of the ju-ju hut? A grisly whisper seemed to tell me that she was but playing with me,

35

as a cat allows a mouse almost to escape, only to be pounced upon again.

"Kirby, what's the matter with you?" I scarcely heard Braxton's anxious voice. "You're sweatin' and shakin' like you had the aggers. What-hey, what you stoppin' for?"

I had not consciously pulled on the rein, but my horse halted, and stood trembling and snorting, before the mouth of a narrow trail which meandered away at right angles from the road we were following-a trail that led north.

"Listen!" I hissed tensely.

"What is it?" Braxton drew a pistol. The brief twilight of the pinelands was deepening into dusk.

"Don't you hear it?" I muttered. "Drums! Drums beating in Goshen!"

"I don't hear nothin'," he mumbled uneasily. "If they was beatin' drums in Goshen you couldn't hear 'em this far away."

"Look there!" my sharp sudden cry made him start. I was pointing down the dim trail, at the figure which stood there in the dusk less than a hundred yards away. There in the dusk I saw her, even made out the gleam of her strange eyes, the mocking smile on her red lips. "Saul Stark's brown wench!" I raved, tearing at my scabbard. "My God, man, are you stone-blind? Don't you see her?"

"I don't see nobody!" he whispered, livid. "What are you talkin' about, Kirby?"

With eyes glaring I fired down the trail, and fired again, and yet again. This time no paralysis gripped my arm. But the smiling face still mocked me from the shadows. A slender, rounded arm lifted, a finger beckoned imperiously; and then she was gone and I was spurring my horse down the narrow trail, blind, dead and dumb, with a sensation as of being caught in a black tide that was carrying me with it as it rushed on to a destination beyond my comprehension.

Dimly I heard Braxton's urgent yells, and then he drew up beside me with a clatter of hoofs, and grabbed my reins, setting my horse back on its haunches. I remember striking at him with my gun-barrel, without realizing what I was doing. All the black rivers of Africa were suring and foaming within my consciousness, roaring into a torrent that was sweeping me down to engulf me in an ocean of doom.

"Kirby, are you crazy? This trail leads to Goshen!"

I shook my head dazedly. The foam of the rushing waters swirled in my brain, and my voice sounded far away. "Go back! Ride for Grimesville! I'm going to Goshen."

"Kirby, you're mad!"

"Mad or sane, I'm going to Goshen this night," I answered dully. I was fully conscious. I knew what I was saying, and what I was doing. I realized the incredible folly of my action, and I realized my inability to help myself. Some shred to sanity impelled me to try to conceal the grisly truth from my companion, to offer a rational reason for my madness. "Saul Stark is in Goshen. He's the one who's responsible for all this trouble. I'm going to kill him. That will stop the uprising before it starts."

He was trembling like a man with the ague.

"Then I'm goin' with you."

"You must go on to Grimesville and warn the people," I insisted, holding to sanity, but feeling a strong urge begin to seize me, an irresistible urge to be in motion-to be riding in the direction toward which I was so horribly drawn.

"They'll be on their guard," he said stubbornly.

"They won't need my warnin'. I'm goin' with you. I don't know what's got in you, but I ain't goin' to let you die alone among these black woods."

I did not argue. I could not. The blind rivers were sweeping me on-on-on! And down the trail, dim in the dusk, I glimpsed a supple figure, caught the gleam of uncanny eyes, the crook of a lifted finger...Then I was in motion, galloping down the trail, and I heard the drum of Braxton's horse's hoofs behind me.

THE DWELLERS IN THE SWAMP

Night fell and the moon shone through the trees, blood-red behind the black branches. The horses were growing hard to manage.

"They got more sense'n us, Kirby," muttered Braxton.

"Panther, maybe," I replied absently, my eyes searching the gloom of the trail ahead.

"Naw, t'ain't. Closer we get to Goshen, the worse they git. And every time we swing nigh to a creek they shy and snort."

The trail had not yet crossed any of the narrow, muddy creeks that criss-crossed that end of Canaan, but several times it had swung so close to one of them that we glimpsed the black streak that was water glinting dully in the shadows of the thick growth. And each time, I remembered, the horses showed signs of fear.

But I had hardly noticed, wrestling as I was with the grisly compulsion that was driving me. Remember, I was not like a man in a hypnotic trance. I was fully aware, fully conscious. Even the daze in which I had seemed to hear the roar of black rivers had passed, leaving my mind clear, my thoughts lucid. And that was the sweating hell of it: to realize my folly clearly and poignantly, but to be unable to conquer it. Vividly I realized that I was riding to torture and death, and leading a faithful friend to the same end. But on I went. My efforts to break the spell that gripped me almost unseated my reason, but on I went. I cannot explain my compulsion, any more than I can explain why a sliver of steel is drawn to a magnet. It was a black power beyond the ring of white man's knowledge; a basic, elemental thing of which formal hypnotism is but scanty crumbs, spilled at random. A power beyond my control was drawing me to Goshen, and beyond; more I cannot explain, any more than the rabbit could explain why the eyes of the swaying serpent draw him into its gaping jaws.

We were not far from Goshen when Braxton's horse unseated its rider, and my own began snorting and plunging.

"They won't go no closer!" gasped Braxton, fighting at the reins.

I swung off, threw the reins over the saddle-horn.

"Go back, for God's sake, Jim! I'm going on afoot."

I heard him whimper an oath, then his horse was galloping after mine, and he was following me on foot. The thought that he must share my doom sickened me, but I could not dissuade him; and ahead of me a supple form was dancing in the shadows, luring me on--on-on...

I wasted no more bullets on that mocking shape. Braxton could not see it, and I knew it was part of my enchantment, no real woman of flesh and blood, but a hell-born will-o'-

40

the-wisp, mocking me and leading me through the night to a hideous death. A "sending," the people of the Orient, who are wiser than we, call such a thing.

Braxton peered nervously at the black forest walls about us, and I knew his flesh was crawling with the fear of sawedoff shotguns blasting us suddenly from the shadows. But it was no ambush of lead or steel I feared as we emerged into the moonlit clearing that housed the cabins of Goshen.

The double line of log cabins faced each other across the dusty street. One line backed against the bank of Tularoosa Creek. The black stoops almost overhung the black waters. Nothing moved in the moonlight. No lights showed, no smoke oozed up from the stick-and-mud chimneys. It might have been a dead town, deserted and forgotten.

"It's a trap!" hissed Braxton, his eyes blazing slits. He bent forward like a skulking panther, a gun in each hand. "They're layin' for us in them huts!"

Then he cursed, but followed me as I strode down the street. I did not hail the silent huts. I knew Goshen was deserted. I felt its emptiness. Yet there was a contradictory sensation as of spying eyes fixed upon us. I did not try to reconcile these opposite convictions.

"They're gone," muttered Braxton, nervously. "I can't smell 'em. I can always smell niggers, if they're a lot of 'em, or if they're right close. You reckon they've gone to raid Grimesville?"

"No," I muttered. "They're in the House of Damballah."

He shot a quick glance at me.

"That's a neck of land in the Tularoosa about three miles west of here. My grandpap used to talk about it. The niggers held their heathen palavers there back in slave times. You ain't-Kirby-you-

"Listen!" I wiped the icy sweat from my face.

"Listen!"

Through the black woodlands the faint throb of a drum whispered on the wind that glided up the shadowy reaches of the Tularoosa.

Braxton shivered. "It's them, all right. But for, God's sake, Kirby-look out!"

With an oath he sprang toward the houses on the bank of the creek. I was after him just in time to glimpse a dark clumsy object scrambling or tumbling down, the sloping bank into the water. Braxton threw up his long pistol, then lowered it, with a baffled curse. A faint splash marked the disappearance of the creature. The shiny black surface crinkled with spreading ripples.

"What was it?" I demanded.

"A nigger on his all-fours!" swore Braxton. His face was strangely pallid in the moonlight. "He was crouched between them cabins there, watchin' us!"

"It must have been an alligator." What a mystery is the human mind! I was arguing for sanity and logic, I, the blind victim of a compulsion beyond sanity and logic. "A nigger would have to come up for air."

"He swum under the water and come up in the shadder of the bresh where we couldn't see him," maintained Braxton. "Now he'll go warn Saul Stark."

"Never mind!" The pulse was thrumming in my temples again, the roar of foaming water rising irresistibly in my brain. "I'm going-straight through the swamp. For the last time, go back!"

"No! Sane or mad, I'm goin' with you!"

The pulse of the drum was fitful, growing more distinct as we advanced. We struggled through jungle-thick growth; tangled vines tripped us; our boots sank in scummy mire. We were entering the fringe of the swamp which grew deeper and denser until it culminated in the uninhabitable morass where the Tularoosa flowed into Black River, miles farther to the west.

The moon had not yet set, but the shadows were black under the interlacing branches with their mossy beards. We plunged into the first creek we must cross, one of the many muddy streams flowing into the Tularoosa. The water was only thigh-deep, the moss-clogged bottom fairly firm. My foot felt the edge of a sheer drop, and I warned Braxton: "Look out for a deep hole; keep right behind me."

His answer was unintelligible. He was breathing heavily, crowding close behind me. Just as I reached the sloping bank and pulled myself up by the slimy, projecting roots, the water was violently agitated behind me. Braxton cried out incoherently, and hurled himself up the bank, almost upsetting me. I wheeled, gun in hand, but saw only the black water seething and whirling, after his thrashing rush through it.

"What the devil, Jim?"

"Somethin' grabbed me!" he panted. "Somethin' out of the deep hole. I tore loose and busted up the bank. I tell you, Kirby, something's follerin' us! Somethin' that swims under the water."

"Maybe it was that nigger you saw. These swamp people swim like fish. Maybe he swam up under the water to try to drown you."

He shook his head, staring at the black water, gun in hand.

"It smelt like a nigger, and the little I saw of it looked like a nigger. But it didn't feel like any kind of a human."

"Well, it was an alligator then," I muttered absently as I turned away. As always when I halted, even for a moment, the roar of peremptory and imperious rivers shook the foundations of my reason.

He splashed after me without comment. Scummy puddles rose about our ankles, and we stumbled over mossgrown cypress knees. Ahead of us there loomed another, wider creek, and Braxton caught my arm.

"Don't do it, Kirby!" he gasped. "If we go into that water, it'll git us sure!"

"What?"

"I don't know. Whatever it was that flopped down that bank back there in Goshen. The same thing that grabbed me in that creek back yonder. Kirby, let's go back."

"Go back?" I laughed in bitter agony. "I wish to God I could! I've got to go on. Either Saul Stark or I must die before dawn."

He licked dry lips and whispered. "Go on, then; I'm with you, come heaven or hell." He thrust his pistol back into its scabbard, and drew a long keen knife from his boot. "Go ahead!"

I climbed down the sloping bank and splashed into the water that rose to my hips. The cypress branches bent a gloomy, moss-trailing arch over the creek. The water was black as midnight. Braxton was a blur, toiling behind me. I gained the first shelf of the opposite bank and paused, in water knee-deep, to turn and look back at him.

Everything happened at once, then. I saw Braxton halt short, staring at something on the bank behind me. He cried out, whipped out a gun and fired, just as I turned. In the flash of the gun I glimpsed a supple form reeling backward, a brown face fiendishly contorted. Then in the momentary blindness that followed the flash, I heard Jim Braxton scream.

Sight and brain cleared in time to show me a sudden swirl of the murky water, a round, black object breaking the surface behind Jim-and then Braxton gave a strangled cry and went under with a frantic thrashing and splashing. With an incoherent yell I sprang into the creek, stumbled and went to my knees, almost submerging myself. As I struggled up I saw Braxton's head, now streaming blood, break the surface for an instant, and I lunged toward it. It went under and another head appeared in its place, a shadowy black head. I stabbed-at it ferociously, and my knife cut only the blank water as the thing dipped out of sight.

I staggered from the wasted force of the blow, and when I righted myself, the water lay unbroken about me. I called Jim's name, but there was no answer. Then panic laid a cold hand on me, and I splashed to the bank, sweating and trembling. With the water no higher than my knees I halted and waited, for I knew not what. But presently, down the creek a short distance, I made out a vague object lying in the shallow water near the shore.

I waded to it, through the clinging mud and crawling vines. It was Jim Braxton, and he was dead. It was not the wound in his head which had killed him. Probably he had struck a submerged rock when he was dragged under. But the marks of strangling fingers showed black on his throat.

At the sight a nameless horror oozed out of that black swamp and coiled itself clammily about my soul; for no human fingers ever left such marks as those.

I had seen a head rise in the water, a head that looked like that of a Negro, though the features had been indistinct in the darkness. But no man, white or black, ever possessed the fingers that had crushed the life out of Jim Braxton. The distant drum grunted as if in mockery.

I dragged the body up on the bank and left it. I could not linger longer, for the madness was foaming in my brain again, driving me with white-hot spurs. But as I climbed the bank, I found blood on the bushes, and was shaken by the implication.

I remembered the figure I had seen staggering in the flash of Braxton's gun. She had been there, waiting for me on the bank, then-not a spectral illusion, but the woman herself, in flesh and blood! Braxton had fired at her, and wounded her. But the wound could not have been mortal; for no corpse lay among the bushes, and the grim hypnosis that dragged me onward was unweakened. Dizzily I wondered if she could be killed by mortal weapons.

The moon had set. The starlight scarcely penetrated the interwoven branches. No more creeks barred my way, only shallow streams, through which I splashed with sweating haste. Yet I did not expect to be attacked. Twice the dweller in the depths had passed me by to attack my companion.

In icy despair I knew I was being saved for the grimmer fate. Each stream I crossed might be hiding the monster that killed Jim Braxton. Those creeks were all connected in a network of winding waterways. It could follow me easily. But my horror of it was less than the horror of the jungle-born magnetism that lurked in a witch-woman's eyes.

And as I stumbled through the tangled vegetation, I heard the drum rumbling ahead of me, louder and louder, a demoniacal mockery. Then a human voice mingled with its mutter, in a long-drawn cry of horror and agony that set every fiber of me quivering with sympathy. Sweat coursed down my clammy flesh; soon my own voice might be lifted like that, under unnamable torture. But on I went, my feet moving like automatons, apart from my body, motivated by a will not my own.

The drum grew loud, and a fire glowed among the black trees. Presently, crouching among the bushes, I stared across the stretch of black water that separated Tae from a nightmare scene. My halting there was as compulsory as the rest of my actions had been. Vaguely I knew the stage for horror had been set, but the time for my entry upon it was not yet. When the time had come, I would receive my summons.

A low, wooded island split the black creek, connected with the shore opposite me by a narrow neck of land. At its lower end the creek split into a network of channels threading their way among hummocks and rotting logs and mossgrown, vine-tangled clumps of trees. Directly across from my refuge the shore of the island was deeply indented by an arm of open, deep black water. Bearded trees walled a small clearing, and partly hid a hut. Between the but and the shore burned afire that sent up weird twisting snake-tongues of green flames. Scores of black people squatted under the shadows of the overhanging branches. When the green fire lit their faces it lent them the appearance of drowned corpses.

In the midst of the glade stood a giant Negro, an awesome statue in black marble. He was clad in ragged trousers, but on his head was a band of beaten gold set with a huge red jewel, and on his feet were barbaric sandals. His features reflected titanic vitality no less than his huge body. But he was all Negro-flaring nostrils, thick lips, ebony skin. I knew I looked upon Saul Stark, the conjure man.

He was regarding something that lay in the sand before him, something dark and bulky that moaned feebly. Presently, lifting his head, he rolled out a sonorous invocation across the black waters. From the blacks huddled under the trees there came a shuddering response, like a wind wailing through midnight branches. Both invocation and response were framed in an unknown tongue-a guttural, primitive language.

Again he called out, this time a curious high-pitched wail. A shuddering sigh swept the black people. All eyes were fixed on the dusky water. And presently an object rose slowly from the depths. A sudden trembling shook me. It looked like the head of a Negro. One after another it was followed by similar objects until five heads reared above the black, cypress-shadowed water. They might have been five Negroes submerged except for their heads-but I knew this was not so. There was something diabolical here. Their silence, motionlessness, their whole aspect was unnatural. From the trees came the hysterical sobbing of women, and someone whispered a man's name.

Then Saul Stark lifted his hands, and the five heads silently sank out of sight. Like a ghostly whisper I seemed to hear the voice of the African witch: "He pals them in the swamp!"

Stark's deep voice rolled out across the narrow water: "And now the Dance of the Skull, to make the conjer sure!"

What had the witch said? "Hidden among the trees You shall watch the dance of the Skull!"

The drum struck up again, growling and rumbling. The blacks swayed on their haunches, lifting a wordless chant. Saul Stark paced measuredly about the figure on the sand, his arms weaving cryptic patterns. Then he wheeled and faced toward the other end of the glade. By some sleight of hand he now grasped a grinning human skull, and this he cast upon the wet sand beyond the body. "Bride of Damballah!" he thundered. "The sacrifice awaits!"

There was an expectant pause; the chanting sank. All eyes were glued on the farther end of the glade. Stark stood waiting, and I saw him scowl as if puzzled. Then as he opened his mouth to repeat the call, a barbaric figure moved out of the shadows.

At the sight of her a chill shuddering shook me. For a moment she stood motionless, the firelight glinting on her gold ornaments, her head hanging on her breast. A tense silence reigned and I saw Saul Stark staring at her sharply. She seemed to be detached, somehow, standing aloof and withdrawn, head bent strangely.

Then, as if rousing herself, she began to sway with a jerky rhythm, and presently whirled into the mazes of a dance that was ancient when the ocean drowned the black kings of Atlantis. I cannot describe it. It was bestiality and diabolism set to motion, framed in a writhing, spinning whirl of posturing and gesturing that would have appalled a dancer of the Pharaohs. And that cursed skull danced with her; rattling and clashing on the sand, it bounded and spun like a live thing in time with her leaps and prancings.

But there was something amiss. I sensed it. Her arms hung limp, her drooping head swayed. Her legs bent and faltered, making her lurch drunkenly and out of time. A murmur rose from the people, and bewilderment etched Saul Stark's black countenance. For the domination of a conjure man is a thing hinged on a hair-trigger. Any trifling dislocation of formula or ritual may disrupt the whole web of his enchantment.

As for me, I felt the perspiration freeze on my flesh as I watched the grisly dance. The unseen shackles that bound me to that gyrating she-devil were strangling, crushing me. I knew she was approaching a climax, when she would summon me from my hiding-place, to wade through the black waters to the House of Damballah, to my doom.

Now she whirled to a floating stop, and when she halted, poised on her toes, she faced toward the spot where I lay hidden, and I knew that she could see me as plainly as if I stood in the open; knew, too, somehow, that only she knew of my presence. I felt myself toppling on the edge of the abyss. She raised her head and I saw the flame of her eyes, even at that distance. Her face was lit with awful triumph. Slowly she raised her hand, and I felt my limbs begin to jerk in response to that terrible magnetism. She opened her mouth-

But from that open mouth sounded only a choking gurgle, and suddenly her lips were dyed crimson. And suddenly, without warning, her knees gave way and she pitched headlong into the sands.

And as she fell, so I too fell, sinking into the mire.

Something burst in my brain with a shower of flame. And then I was crouching among the trees, weak and trembling, but with such a sense of freedom and lightness of limb as I never dreamed a man could experience. The black spell that gripped me was broken; the foul incubus lifted from my soul. It was as if light had burst upon a night blacker than African midnight.

At the fall of the girl a wild cry rose from the blacks, and they sprang up, trembling on the verge of panic. I saw their rolling white eyeballs, their bared teeth glistening in the firelight. Saul Stark had worked their primitive natures up to a pitch of madness, meaning to turn this frenzy, at the proper time, into a fury of battle. It could as easily turn into an hysteria of terror. Stark shouted sharply at them.

But just then the girl in a last convulsion, rolled over on the wet sand, and the firelight shone on a round hole between her breasts, which still oozed crimson. Jim Braxton's bullet had found its mark.

From the first I had felt that she was not wholly human; some black jungle spirit sired her, lending her the abysmal subhuman vitality that made her what she was. She had said that neither death nor hell could keep her from the Dance of the Skull. And, shot through the heart and dying, she had come through the swamp from the creek where she had received her death-wound to the House of Damballah. And the Dance of the Skull had been her death dance.

Dazed as a condemned man just granted a reprieve, at first I hardly grasped the meaning of the scene that now unfolded before me.

The blacks were in a frenzy. In the sudden, and to them inexplicable, death of the sorceress they saw a fearsome portent. They had no way of knowing that she was dying when she entered the glade. To them, their prophetess and priestess had been struck down under their very eyes, by an invisible death. This was magic blacker than Saul Stark's wizardry-and obviously hostile to them.

Like fear-maddened cattle they stampeded. Howling, screaming, tearing at one another they blundered through the trees, heading for the neck of land and the shore beyond. Saul Stark stood transfixed, heedless of them as he stared down at the brown girl, dead at last. And suddenly I came to myself, and with my awakened manhood came cold fury and the lust to kill. I drew a gun, and aiming in the uncertain firelight, pulled the trigger. Only a click answered me. The powder in the cap-and-ball pistols was wet.

Saul Stark lifted his head and licked his lips. The sounds of flight faded in the distance, and he stood alone in the glade. His eyes rolled whitely toward the black woods around him. He bent, grasped the man-like object that lay on the sand, and dragged it into the hut. The instant he vanished I started toward the island, wading through the narrow channels at the lower end. I had almost reached the shore when a mass of driftwood gave way with me and I slid into a deep hole.

Instantly the water swirled about me, and a head rose beside me; a dim face was close to mine-the face of a Negrothe face of Tunk Bixby. But now it was inhuman; as expressionless and soulless as that of a catfish; the face of a being no longer human, and no longer mindful of its human origin.

Slimy, misshapen fingers gripped my throat, and I drove my knife into the sagging mouth. The features vanished in a wave of blood; mutely the thing sank out of sight, and I hauled myself up the bank, under the thick bushes.

Stark had run from his hut, a pistol in his hand. He was staring wildly about, alarmed by the noise he had heard, but I knew he could not see me. His ashy skin glistened with perspiration. He who had ruled by fear was now ruled by fear. He feared the unknown hand that had slain his mistress; feared the Negroes who had fled him; feared the abysmal swamp which had sheltered him, and the monstrosities he had created. He lifted a weird call that quavered with panic. He called again as only four heads broke the water, but he called in vain.

But the four heads began to move toward the shore and the man who stood there. He shot them one after another. They made no effort to avoid the bullets. They came straight on, sinking one by one. He had fired six shots before the last head vanished. The shots drowned the sounds of my approach. I was close behind him when he turned at last.

I know he knew me; recognition flooded his face and fear went with it, at the knowledge that he had a human being to deal with. With a scream he hurled his empty pistol at me and rushed after it with a lifted knife.

I ducked, parried his lunge and countered with a thrust that bit deep into his ribs. He caught my wrist and I gripped his, and there we strained, breast to breast. His eyes were like a mad dog's in the starlight, his muscles like steel cords.

I ground my heel down on his bare foot, crushing the instep. He howled and lost balance, and I tore my knife hand free and stabbed him in the belly. Blood spurted and he dragged me down with him. I jerked loose and rose, just as he pulled himself up on his elbow and hurled his knife. It sang past my ear, and I stamped on his breast. His ribs caved in under my heel. In a red killing-haze I knelt, jerked back his head and cut his throat from ear to ear.

There was a pouch of dry powder in his belt. Before I moved further I reloaded my pistols. Then I went into the but with a torch. And there I understood the doom the brown witch had meant for me. Tope Sorley lay moaning on a bunk. The transmutation that was to make him a mindless, soulless semi-human dweller in the water was not complete, but his mind was gone. Some of the physical changes had been made-by what godless sorcery out of Africa's black abyss I have no wish to know. His body was rounded and elongated, his legs dwarfed; his feet were flattened and broadened, his fingers horribly long, and webbed. His neck was inches longer than it should be. His features were not altered, but the expression was no more human than that of a great fish. And there, but for the loyalty of Jim Braxton, lay Kirby Buckner. I placed my pistol muzzle against Tope's head in grim mercy and pulled the trigger.

And so the nightmare closed, and I would not drag out the grisly narration. The white people of Canaan never found anything on the island except the bodies of Saul Stark and the brown woman. They think to this day that a swamp negro killed Jim Braxton, after he had killed the brown woman, and that I broke up the threatened uprising by killing Saul Stark. I let them think it. They will never know the shapes the black water of Tularoosa hides. That is a secret I share with the cowed and terror-haunted black people of Goshen and of it neither they nor I have ever spoken.